# The Softest Sleep

## by **Anne Goscinny**

Translated from the French by **Stuart Bell**

Introduced by **Emma Wilson**

Published 2020 by the87press

The 87 Press LTD

87 Stonecot Hill

Sutton

Surrey

SM3 9HJ

www.the87press.com

ISBN: 978-1-9164774-7-6

Design: Stanislava Stoilova [www.sdesign.graphics]

ANNE GOSCINNY is a French novelist and literary critic. She is the author of *Le Bureau des solitudes* (2002), *Le Voleur de mère* (2004), *Le Père éternel* (2006, winner of La Wizo Prize), *Le Banc des soupirs* (2011), *Le bruit des clefs* (2012), *Le sommeil le plus doux* (2016) and *Sous tes baisers* (2017).

STUART BELL is a literary translator. He studied Modern Languages at the University of Cambridge and then as a postgraduate at Birkbeck, University of London. He has previously published the first translation into English of Pascal Bruckner's *They Stole Our Beauty* (2019) and is currently working on translating contemporary French experimental poetry.

EMMA WILSON teaches French at the University of Cambridge and is currently researching on contemporary French women writers and filmmakers. Her books include *Love, Mortality and the Moving Image* (2012) and *The Reclining Nude: Agnès Varda, Catherine Breillat, and Nan Goldin* (2019).

# *Introduction*

Anne Goscinny's *The Softest Sleep* was published in French by Grasset in 2016 and appears here for the first time in English translation. Goscinny has been publishing fiction since 2002, and in 2017 wrote a short memoir, a retrospective letter to her dead father, in a series with NiL editions. She is also a lyricist and wrote songs for the Italian-born French singer Serge Reggiani. Her writing, modest, *sotto voce*, yet infinitely passionate and tender, finds its place in the French literary landscape between fiction and life-writing. Her themes are close to those of Annie Ernaux who has memorialised the death of her parents, her passing affair with a Russian diplomat, and, writing in the same NiL series as Goscinny, her late discovery of the existence of a sister who died before she was born. Contemporary French writing, especially by women, is unequalled in its approach to microhistories of the heart, of the everyday, of family ties, and erotic entanglements. The social world of Goscinny's text is different from Ernaux's, more cushioned, closer to that of another contemporary Laurence Tardieu who writes very moving fiction of death and survival. Yet Goscinny's is also a world of the Jewish diaspora in France, a history of exile and traumatic loss the context and family condition of her writing. *The Softest Sleep* is a novel, yet its themes and scenarios resonate with those of her memoir, indeed those of her various recent texts, each gripping and beautiful in its own right. The novel's appearance in English, in Stuart Bell's supple translation, is a cause of celebration.

The novel takes place in Nice. It starts as a plane lands, arriving here in deep winter, in the midst of Christmas festivities. Jeanne, the first narrator, is travelling with her mother and her dead father's mother. This is a memorial trip to stay in a grand hotel in this Mediterranean city, Nice, with its palms, its Bay of Angels, its Russian cathedral, and the white mansions of Cimiez high above. The city and the sea stretching around it feel as if they are part of a mirage, a place of the past, or of the mind. Jeanne's mother is dying and this trip is her last glimmer of life, her last moments of luxury, of champagne in her hotel bedroom, in 'her place of birth, her childhood home'. This remembered space, revisited by the three women, looks out to the melancholy and interior tranquillity of a Matisse painting.

The Softest Sleep offers a nostalgic and painful account of the relations between three generations of women. Jeanne's grandmother, her father's mother, has survived the pogroms of the Second World War in Ukraine, and the more recent death in France of her only son. She accompanies Jeanne and her mother on this trip as a guarantor of memory and family ties, yet seems ultimately lost in her own world. The filial drama of the novel is between Jeanne and her mother. The Softest Sleep is most poignant in its observations of small details, its understanding of wishfulness and magical thinking. Arriving in Nice, Jeanne's mother is assailed by memories: 'She is twenty; her whole life is ahead of her. She is so pretty.' Jeanne drives slowly along the Promenade des Anglais with its palms, 'to prolong the pleasure of this reunion between her and her childhood'. She speaks of 'this shred of hope' she clings to 'by creating memories to come'. In the hotel, surely the Negresco, 'famous with its pink towers, its name proudly emblazoned across the front', Jeanne's mother unpacks her wardrobes of clothes. Jeanne knows her death is so close, yet she writes: 'She could be staying in Nice for a month, two, for life – the life that's left to live'. This arrival, and optimistic settling in, fosters the illusion that in this different place life might be pursued, the mother might survive. Nice, its palms, the sea, might exist outside the usual, mortal, temporal realm.

The novel is fine and true about the pain of living in memories. As they drink in the hotel room, Jeanne's mother confides: 'Your father was never more alive than in death. Try rebuilding your life when you wake up orgasming at the touch of a long-buried hand you know has turned to dust!' She continues: 'I never fell in love again'. Looking back over her life, Jeanne's mother is between living and dying. Jeanne narrates: 'My mother is sound asleep. As per morning routine, I kiss her softly on the lips to make sure it is only sleep that holds her still'. In their last exchanges, it is as if her mother is preparing her for her orphan future: 'Mourning will be your core'. The novel is excoriating in its reckoning with loss, with the ache of the bone cancer that is killing Jeanne's mother, and with the daughter's intimations of her own bereft life to come. Yet it also offers its distractions from the tenderness, horror and grief of the mother daughter couple at its heart.

Interleaved with Jeanne's narrative passages are the words of Gabriel, a man Jeanne encounters on a park bench as she wanders in Nice, escaping the hotel rooms. Their encounter in this public space of the city is pursed in his apartment where he makes love to her, stroking her body, reflecting that she is so young and frail she might be his child. The novel comes to align these different bodily and emotional intensities, pain and the approach to dying, and desire, love with a stranger found of the streets of the city. A strange tenderness and awe seems to couple the two. It is as if Jeanne's grief and emotional emptiness inspire Gabriel's erotic feeling. If family losses and accounts of erotic attachments have been staple subjects in contemporary French writing, Goscinny here brings the two peculiarly close.

The novel has its own temporal and plot surprises that I will pass over here, but it is worth dwelling on what Gabriel brings to the novel as a counterpoint to its narrative of three women. He voices almost half of the book, a narrative form

3

of crossed male and female narrations. This is a form that Goscinny pursues in her as yet untranslated *Sous tes baisers* from 2017. This text, like *The Softest Sleep*, narrates a love affair between a dominant, seductive man and a woman with different vulnerabilities. Goscinny is radical in, fairly uncritically, showing her characters' desire for a controlling, paternal figure. Making this relation more central than does *The Softest Sleep*, *Sous tes baisers* is extraordinary in its account of falling in love and of the scenarios of desire. Its male protagonist imagines himself as the choreographer of the afternoons he spends with his lover. She is spellbound, a butterfly with new wings. Gabriel, randomly encountered in Nice, allows the masculine, the paternal to enter the novel.

In her memoir addressed to her father, Goscinny contemplates the effect on her life as a heterosexual woman of the loss of her father in her childhood. She writes that she has to learn to be desirable without his gaze to affirm her. Most poignantly she speaks about grieving the Anne she might have become if he hadn't died. She says that sometimes she invokes this other Anne. Goscinny's father was the glorious writer René Goscinny, author most famously of the Astérix books. Anne adored him and was cherished by him before he died of a heart attack, in his own cardiologist's office, when she was nine years old. Since the death of her mother, Goscinny has gone on to look after her father's literary estate. She comments, in her memoir, that it sometimes seems as if she has taken on the role of widow as well as orphan. Her memoir, like *The Softest Sleep*, is rich with details, showing the bereaved daughter buying her father's cologne to remember him, reading his books as if she is doing her homework.

Goscinny has become an important author in her own right, beyond her father's shadow. She wrote her masters thesis in Paris on the novels of Jean Rhys and it is in this line too that her work can be understood. Like Rhys she is acerbic and lyrical all at once, her characters in love with older men, the encounters erotic and painful, her view of life melancholy and yet always resilient. She finds her perfect translator in Stuart Bell whose sensitive work captures the mood and languor of Goscinny's writing. Bell has previously translated another contemporary French novel on obsession and desire, Pascal Bruckner's *They Stole Our Beauty* (the87press 2019), and he is currently translating contemporary French experimental poetry. Bell, a passionate reader of Proust, Alain Robbe-Grillet, and Marguerite Duras, a teacher of French language and literature, an author himself, is well-placed to do justice to the writing of Goscinny, a novelist of infinite delicacy whose works richly deserve a wider readership.

Professor Emma Wilson
University of Cambridge

'Each and every one of us ends up thinking he is a character caught up in God knows what adventure, even a very simple one, yet we ought to know that we are the whole story, not only this character. We are the forest in which he walks, the outlaw that mistreats him, the disturbance all around, the people passing by, the colour of things, the sounds. Do you understand?'

ALESSANDRO BARICCO (Mr Gwyn)

My daughter, my child
I see the time is coming
When you will leave me
To change seasons
To change home
To change habits
I think about it every evening
Looking back over
Your childhood that wants
To cast off the ropes
And leaves me with the taste
Of a guitar chord

EDDY MARNAY / RAYMOND BERNARD
(for SERGE REGGIANI)

# *The day before*

## Jeanne

The plane passes over the water and lands. My mother is dozing, undisturbed by the jolting of the aircraft, and my grandmother is laughing. There are three of us. Tonight is Christmas Eve. We are staying in Nice for just three days. Still, my mother has packed a large suitcase. A suitcase to last her until spring, or to a time when she won't go home. Maybe she knows; surely she knows that for her next trip she needs no luggage.

In true Mary Poppins style, my grandmother has brought only a small bag I wouldn't be surprised to find filled with gherkins, stuffed carp, or kasha.

'You see my darling, you know where you've come from, but you don't know where you're going!'

As we disembark, my mother smiles. Here we are in Nice: her place of birth, her childhood home. In this precise moment, the future, or what is left of it, becomes clear.

Slight, dignified, wearing a bottle-green crepe dress, my grandmother takes short, sure steps. She smiles endlessly, and ever watchful, she greets new arrivals who can't see her.

My mother's face lights up. I am not in these memories. And it doesn't matter: I am not a memory.

I know she's thinking about her father, this tideless sea, Colette and Pierrot, their never-ending games of Mah-Jong. I understand, but won't say anything. I'm driving the hire car; Nice opens up before us. She wants to binge again on palm trees and the Mediterranean. A shadow passes we don't see.

She is talkative in the car. Tells me about things I already know by heart: her scooter, turning sixteen, Michel who was so handsome and Marie-France whom she loved so much. Her childhood home in the Cimiez neighbourhood and her mother who never got over the local man she fell in love with. Their whole affair was straight out of a Jacques Brel love song...

'She started hating pastis and olives, the sun and the Promenade des Anglais. She shut herself away and made a shrine to her home country. She used to kneel at the altar in our living room, decorated in fine detail: a glass bottle filled with sand taken from the beach at Knokke-le-Zoute, photos of its seawall and nature parks, and of course, a portrait of Leopold III. There's no denying she became a recluse... There were no onion tarts in our house, but we did have Belgian stew. I grew up in Nice, on the North Sea coast.'

I'm listening, trying to pretend I'm hearing it all for the first time. The scooter, the Mah-Jong, Michel's eyes.

Discreet and silent, my grandmother (my father's mother) is joining us. She survived the persecution of the Jews in the Second World War and the death of her only son. Now she laughs at everything. She lives only in the moment, as though she has forgotten the rest. Surely she knows I'm her granddaughter and my mother is her son's wife. But that's all. Sometimes I tell myself she plays at being senile. Because it's useful, because that way, smiling is all that is expected of her.

Before, she used to tell the same story, on repeat, about how the Tsar's men destroyed her shtetl, entering houses on horseback and burning them. And each time she recalled, without hatred or resentment, how they started with hers: a privilege reserved for the rabbi's family.

'Hatred takes time. I had a family to start, a village to rebuild inside me, my father's house to reconstruct, somewhere else, in the place where everything starts over.'

She saved three objects: a seven-armed silver candelabrum, a marble clock, and a breadknife.

Without her this journey would be meaningless. I needed to bridge this destroyed yet undying world and the uncertain future in which it won't be houses that are consumed but organs instead. She will ease the passage. In keeping these three objects she has carried all her life, my grandmother has clung to time, a weapon, and the light.

I wanted her to come along and had no trouble convincing her. Ever since she has been elsewhere, I talk to her every day; sometimes she replies with only a signal, but she always lets me know she has heard. Other times she stays silent, or rather, silence saves her from my interruptions. Now she can choose to speak or not. A perk not of age but of another world.

'This is pointless,' my mother would have said, had I sprung her mother-in-law on her as a last-minute surprise, part angel, part escapee. 'She's going to be a nuisance,' she'd have said.

But a smile is never a nuisance. It is vital, necessary.

While my mother is going to die, here, tomorrow, the day after, while she won't remember this summer to come, my grandmother has crossed lands and the century. No doubt she doesn't remember who she is, or where she is, yet from the world that's now hers, she loves us. Maybe she thinks my mother is her daughter and it's her responsibility to marry her off. And like any good matchmaker, she will spread the word far and wide.

My mother is laughing as she talks. She is twenty; her whole life is ahead of her. She is so pretty. I wish the hotel was further away, very far, that the long line of palm trees would never end. I drive slowly to prolong the pleasure of this reunion between her and her childhood, between her and this shred of hope I cling to by creating memories to come.

Eventually the hotel rises up before us, tall and famous with its pink towers, its name proudly emblazoned across the front.

I help her out of the car. I know she is suffering. Yet in this moment, she isn't in pain. The sight of her childhood, her youth, has done her more good than a morphine injection. At reception, they hand her the key to her room. She is like a young girl pretending, playing the pilgrim, come not to end her life but to start all over again. She throws a pebble she imagines she found on a hopscotch stretching from birth to happiness. She forgets – I see it – the timespan of three days. She forgets her days are numbered; she forgets the shadow and its whispers.

Elegant, clutching her bag, my grandmother trails behind, smiling. She is wearing her pearl necklace and engagement ring. A small diamond set in onyx. Over her dress, a shawl whose patterned flowers must have once been buds. Look at them, now open; their time has passed, yet they haven't wilted.

We take the lift. Our suitcases will follow. My mother explores her room, her eyes wide in the bathroom with its gigantic, golden bathtub. Our rooms are adjoining. We step into mine. There is an enormous bed with a faux fur bedspread and a classic bathtub, regular-sized and ivory. My mother cries out:

'I want you to have the bigger tub!'

And in that moment I understand she is giving me what she can, all she can, because she no longer has the strength to walk around Nice with me, no energy to take me out to dinner in the city outskirts she loves so much. So she gives me her bathtub. Later she'll watch me soak in its vast, tacky hollow. I'll be like a fox thrown in an Olympic swimming pool! I'll say that to her and she will laugh.

I help my grandmother unpack in her room on the same floor. Opening her bag, she smiles. I look for her son in her eyes. And sometimes I find him.

The days to come are going to be bleak. I say nothing. I know she knows. She sits down, like a patient in a waiting room, alert and upright. She pays no attention to the sea or the palms; she is in Ukraine, Paris, Argentina. She is wherever her nonstop life has come to a standstill, wherever her nonstop life has restarted. I kiss her on the forehead and leave her to the wall of gherkin jars she has built around herself. A strange self-defence, alongside the candelabrum, the standstill clock and the breadknife.

The suitcases arrive. My mother doesn't want help unpacking, so I leave her to her own devices. I open the sketchbook I take everywhere with me and start drawing. My pencil is moving in search of her. She smiles as if being photographed. Her face appears, and I add in the hair she no longer has. She places her clothes carefully on the shelves, hangs up her blouses and trousers. She has even brought two or three dresses. Her scarves have their own drawer. She could be staying in Nice for a month, two, for life – the life that's left to live.

'My trousers go here, I'll put jumpers there. In that drawer my pyjamas. My socks there, my tee shirts there. My linen blouses higher up. Look: I'm going to put my books in the night table drawer. Get rid of that Bible! It's crazy how hotels force Bibles on you in bedside tables. I'll sleep just fine without a hymn sheet for the last rites. Oh yes, my scarves! I know my hair will grow back, but these furry tufts are ridiculous. There now – this will last me until spring! Summertime calls for two pairs of loose trousers and a bathing suit. But summer is far away… I've just realised: "Summer" sounds like "summit". Help me lie down. I have to rest for a moment.'

On the bedside table, books are stacked next to her medicine bag. In the bathroom, she lays out her things. Her perfume bottle, one or two face creams, mascara, lipstick.

She is at home. As night closes in, she is carried back to childhood.

In my room, my own set-up is more ordinary, less precise, much less refined. I'm carefree, like the young who know that the important things are waiting beyond the horizon.

It's December 24th.

'Let's kick off Christmas in style!' she tells me.

I can't stop myself veiling everything she says, suggests and implies in a shroud of last-evers. A black gauze sieve that lets light pass through in order to finely filter it.

The hotel restaurant is closed. She doesn't have the strength to venture into town. She rings Colette, her best friend from Nice, and tells her we are coming over for dinner.

I slip out for a few minutes to check on my grandmother. I was worried about her spending Christmas Eve alone, but she smiles and says:

'Don't worry about me, my love. I don't need anything.'

Her bed was untouched, the shutters open, the curtains held in place by overly-ornate tiebacks. She was staring at her clock whose motionless hands looked like two arrows pointing to midday, midnight, or the sky.

I wanted to touch her forehead softly as a sign of tenderness, but in the shadows my hands met with only thin air, emptiness, silence.

Colette opens the door. My mother is mad with joy to be seeing her again. They kiss with all the warmth of friends who know this will be the last reunion.

She sits down in an armchair, or rather falls into it. She doesn't want anything to eat; a glass of red will do. Alone with Colette in the kitchen, I fall apart. She takes me in her arms. We come back to the living room where my mother has fallen asleep for a moment, ashen and tense.

We savour each moment of the evening.

'Remember when you read tarot cards, Colette? I think I was in love with Michel! I loved being alive. I know it's the end. Don't tell me otherwise. Death is sniffing at me. It's all around me. I don't care about dying. But who will be there for Jeanne? I know, I know, she's grown up! Is there any red left in the bottle? Thank you. No, I'm not afraid of what's waiting for me. I'm not scared any more. I spent many nights shaking, terrified, thinking about the coffin. But now I tell myself I'm my own coffin thanks to this illness that's eating away at me, sucking and swallowing me up. Actually, it'll be more comfortable! See, I've loved everything in this life. Even my unhappiness that proved daily I was still alive. I've loved parties, travel, dogs. I've loved making myself look beautiful for a man. I've loved the opera and concerts. I've loved improvising dinners and bringing people together who'd never have met otherwise. Today I'm happy to be sitting here, in your home, in this town, prey to the mistral and its promises.'

She dozes off once more, wakes up, looks at me, says again how happy she is to be back in Nice, then dives back into sleep, a trial-run coma.

Colette promises she will drop in to see us at the hotel the following day, or the one after at the latest.

We head back. She perks up in the car and tries counting the palms. In this moment, she is my child. She is babbling away, and for the duration of the journey, it seems she has forgotten her illness.

Christmas Eve night is here, more dense and mysterious than in religious imagery. No cradle, no Messiah, only cancer and a room.

'The night isn't over yet, Jeanne! Have them send up a bottle of champagne… I want to toast to the end of this year, to the coming one that'll see me off, to all these palms that'll outlive me, to my childhood, and to you and your love life!'

The waiter who brings the champagne could pass for one of the three wise men. Now we are lying side by side on the bed. Secrets make way for more secrets. I've never felt more free. I tell her about the man I like and she smiles knowingly.

'I loved your father passionately. When he died I thought I would go mad. But you know, thankfully this cancer came along to distract me. Chemo side effects haven't left much time for tears. Men have come and gone during my life – none have stayed. Do you remember? The only one I couldn't let go was my husband's ghost. Is there any champagne left? Your father was never more alive than in death. Try rebuilding your life when you wake up orgasming at the touch of a long-buried hand you know has turned to dust! Once, when you were still young, you caught me sitting at the table with Scrabble letter tiles scattered all around me, a glass at the ready. You laughed it off. I never dared tell you I was trying to communicate with your father... except the glass didn't move an inch, so I ended up turning it back over, poured a glass of red and toasted to my dead husband who obviously wasn't in a talkative mood. I never fell in love again. Open that half bottle of champagne in the mini bar and pour me a glass. How can you hope to make love when you look down and see your wig and artificial breast lying there by your feet? Huh? How can you? But in the end, you know, I don't miss it. What I do miss is the idea of a certain tenderness, a hand running through my hair, real or fake. Yes, it's the longing behind the gestures I miss more than the gestures themselves. Go and fetch my cigarettes.'

We make plans for the following days, then venture into more uncertain territory, planning for the weeks ahead. Rejuvenated by the champagne, we talk about the beauty of Provence in spring, how satisfied she will feel trimming the bay trees in the house she just bought.

'You know, happiness for me would be watching the shade grow beneath the Virginia creeper I planted in front of the kitchen two years ago. See, I thought up a slogan for you: happiness is simple as a shady spot. What do you reckon? You haven't a clue how it feels to plant a shrub, lavender or roses, not knowing whether you'll live to see the first flowers or pick the first fruits. That's why I plant radishes. Have you noticed I plant radishes? Because there's nothing to see in any case! Of course, you can't have a garden filled only with radishes. But it's a real shame. It's the lot of a cancerous landscaper. Here, let's toast to my future career with this nice cold little bottle of vodka.'

Life is here, within reach, turnip or lavender-coloured. The words chosen outweigh reality. I have this night to promise her a future, to create a life for her to come. I talk to her about the children I'll have that she'll be proud of, my love for painting that might turn into a career.

This is better than any treatment: talking about her garden, her pergola so thick and vast, one day it will cover all Vaucluse in shade. Tonight, sharing my dreams has won a battle. She falls asleep, happy, with all the ease of an innocent who doesn't know what day it is.

Conscious this is a fragile sleep, I gently close her bedroom door. I cross the hallway and follow the curving lines in the carpet leading to my grandmother. I tread the woven coloured threads, arms folded across my chest, balancing my weight like a tightrope walker. Beneath my feet, I picture a precipice. The path before me, if I follow it without faltering, saves me from death.

The curtains still aren't drawn. The light is switched off. I know she is sitting where I left her. Her pearls seem to glow and carve a smile into the night.

I'm going to bed too, after a few lengths of breaststroke in my golden bathtub.

# December 24th

## Gabriel

Why does Christmas Eve make everyone so anxious? Why is unhappiness so much more palpable this night? For some, this comes through loneliness, for others it is feeling misunderstood. We come together to tear each other apart. Hélène and I arrived in Nice this afternoon. We could have stayed in Paris. Nobody is waiting in this house. It belonged to Hélène's grandparents; her happiest childhood memories were made here. But ghosts from the past are never welcoming hosts. There will be four of us; the twins will arrive tonight, each with a long list of complaints and critiques. They are nearly thirty now, old enough to stop blaming their parents for their woes. But they are different. They tell me I work too hard, neglect their mother, forget their birthdays, even though it's fairly simple: one date for both. The prospect of this evening doesn't fill me with joy. Following a purely ceremonial yet violent trial, carried out in the name of justice for a family faced with dictatorship, I'll be found guilty of all wrongdoings. And instead of talking to me, they will draw up a list of everything I haven't done. Then there is this house in which I've never felt welcome, despite my considerable efforts to shape it, trying to improve our life here by adding a bathroom here, a television there. But there was no fooling it:

'You cannot buy me. I want you to embrace my history. I want your compassion. Save your gifts for your children; I don't want your false tokens of affection. I tolerate you because I know that one day long ago, not far from here, you sealed your fate. Way back then, a few streets past Old Town, across the port, a memory was made: the most beautiful in a young woman's life. I'm over a hundred-and-fifty years old. I am sustained by what I know; this is what connects us to you humans. What link is there between man and stone if not the sharing of memories?'

That's how Hélène's house spoke to me, tolerating but never accepting me.

I stopped trying to appease it. I can't measure up. Guilty of not knowing how to love Hélène, not having understood or gone after it. Its stony shell slipped through my fingers that made no attempt to hold on. Still, its walls will outlive me and hear newer promises, fresher criticisms than these.

We sit down to eat. Hélène is sad, withdrawing more and more from the world around her, and the twins, too busy squabbling, forget I'm there. I open an excellent bottle of wine I'll drink alone. My wife's strict dieting means she only drinks when occasion calls for it, and as for the children, they prefer the speedy effects of other alcohols.

Hoping the presents will lighten the mood, I give mine to Hélène, just like countless excuses throughout the year. To the twins collapsed on the couch I give the customary envelope, quickly discarded after barely-audible comments, such as: 'How tight-fisted can you get? Could he be any more stingy?'

Hélène disappears, in turn, then comes back with presents labelled for me. She must have asked the kids for help buying them. 'Oh, thank you my darling.' She doesn't speak, kisses me absently, and clears the table, wiping away all trace of this dark evening.

The children go to bed without saying a word. Hélène sits in front of me, then summons the strength to cry.

'For God's sake Hélène! Give yourself a break. I don't know what to say, these diets are no good for you. There comes an age when you have to learn to accept yourself and stop trying to fight nature. You are fine as you are. Stop torturing yourself. You're only happy when you paint. Go get your brushes and smile for me. I can't stand being the bad one any more, the root of all evil, the one who never does enough. What about you, Hélène? How do you spend your days? What have you done with your life? You paint those lines but the routes lead nowhere... Why don't you just get on your bike and ride them to hell!'

Drinking makes me cruel. I forget Hélène is ill.

Obviously, my words didn't help. She got up and went to the guest room. I'm guessing she took one of those fast-acting sleeping pills. I finished tidying up and closed the shutters. Before turning in for the night, I opened the door to the bedroom she claimed for herself long ago. She'd fallen asleep on the covers without even disturbing the bedspread. I watched her for a while, searching for the young woman I'd once longed for.

# The morning

## Jeanne

My mother is sound asleep. As per morning routine, I kiss her softly on the lips to make sure it is only sleep that holds her still. Reassured, I go downstairs for breakfast.

She is still sleeping when I get back. This gives me time to check on my grandmother who is busy counting her jars of gherkins. I catch her staring at the bathtub, muttering something about carp in this old Côte d'Azur palace.

'Did you sleep well?'

'You know, my treasure, dreams are the best part of sleep. And dreams help you remember. One detail triggers another, which in turn unearths whatever your memory has buried. So deep, in fact, that sometimes it's only upon waking you remember the features of a face whose shape you'd almost forgotten, if not its very existence. I no longer need sleep to dream. You see, last night I was back in Khodorkov in Ukraine. I was playing in the yard at home with my sisters Olga and Freiga. Meyer and Lev, the twins, weren't yet born. My mother wore a scarf to cover her hair and was sprinkling buckwheat into a cooking pot of boiling water. My father wasn't there. As every other day, he was teaching the village children. I was arguing with Olga again; she was cheating and wouldn't admit it. You see, my treasure, I'm no longer a slave to time, the great architect of forgetting. Today I am however you want to see me. I'm your *Bubbale*, and you are my *Catzele*. Come into my arms.'

Her smile makes me want to discover the world. So I decide to go for a walk in this town I know so little about.

It is mild outside. Nice is opening its presents. The streets are deserted. I walk wrapped up in a coat that's too big for me. All I can think about is my mother, her life of pain. I know the bracket is closing on us like a trap rigged with a time bomb. I picture the half circle that marks the bracket moving dangerously close to the place where it opened. The only space left to inhabit is the gap through which air passes before the circle closes, ever-forming and unstoppable. It's up to me to give it everlasting colour, a pair of tomorrow eyes.

Driven forward by the wind, or by nothing, my stroll takes me into a leafy park. I sit on a bench and unbutton my coat. I breathe. Three pastels and my sketchbook are poised to capture the blue, green and ochre. Meanwhile, my mother is fading. Cancer is filling a suitcase with jumbled up rags, putting on its jacket and sunglasses, ready to go incognito. The cancer has gone. Better yet: it never came. I picture it in a taxi, on a motorbike, on a plane. I see it on a train, a boat, hopping onto a quayside or picking up its luggage in an airport. Anyway, I see it everywhere but I don't want it here, in this Nice hotel, curled up beside my sleeping mother.

I let go of the fantasy of a life without fixed end.

That's when I notice this man. He is close by, sitting on another bench. He must be around forty, maybe more. He looks at me. I have to focus to stop myself staring back. A Christmas loner. A guy who doesn't have custody of his kids this year; he will see them on New Year's Eve instead. One of those who promises his mistress he won't grow old with his wife, then whispers softly into his wife's ear that nothing could ruin the life they've built together.

I won't look at him.

I think about my mother who must be waking up now, alone, worried, in pain. She appeals in secret to God, Saint Rita of Cascia, Saint Tumour. She swears she doesn't believe in anything, but I know, some nights, alcohol helps her pray. An ashen faith, eager but desperate, at 13 degrees.

He gets up.

She is going to call room service and have them send up coffee and grapefruit juice. She will take her first daily round of medications. Gets back into bed, slowly. She knows she could be broken by the slightest unplanned movement, as a fragile object breaks unexpectedly. She is looking for her portable radio. Tunes into any station as long as there is a voice to drown out the anxiety. She doesn't cry in the mornings. Used up her tears falling asleep.

The coffee arrives. Leave it there, on the bed. Thank you. She looks for her glasses, finds them perched on a book on the floor. She is reading *Adieu, Volodya*. No sugar in the coffee. She takes up only a tiny portion of the bed, never touching the other side. She could use it to line up her glasses, books, medications. But no. She doesn't want anything or anyone. If her husband were here, all he could do is lie beside her.

He sits down beside me.

She opens the newspaper, and the coffee is too strong. Looks first for her horoscope. 'LIBRA: Merry Christmas Libran friends! Make the most of today, surrounded by loved ones. Go with the flow. A surprise could mean delights are in store for you!' Then the forecast: 'In the south-east, a gleaming sunshine.' She straightens out the paper, having started at the end, and glances at the headlines and photographs.

I get up.

The day is beginning. It must be lunchtime. As every other morning, she'll take the same long, expectant soak in the tub. She imagines the water has healing power. When she climbs in, she hopes. Eventually she'll get out, tired from relaxation, disappointed. A pair of jeans, a tee shirt and a jumper later, she'll collapse into her bedroom armchair, exhausted.

'Stay.'

He is handsome. His voice moves me. I sit back down on the bench ungracefully. Echoing my mother's tiredness,

I'm overcome with exhaustion.

He tells me his name is Gabriel. I take a better look at him, then focus on my shoelaces.

'My name is Jeanne.'

# December 25<sup>th</sup>

## Gabriel

I dropped my wife and children off at the airport early in the morning.

The gift-exchange ceremony took place last night. Unchanging, uneasy. A tie, a travel bag. Pyjamas and suede gloves. A Prévert poetry collection and tickets to a musical in Châtelet. A clean sweep. I gave Hélène a scarf, a bottle of perfume engraved with her initials, and a ticket to the opera in Aix-en-Provence next summer. The children each had their envelope.

Scallop gratin to start, followed by stuffed cockerel and a chunky yule log, washed down with Corton-Charlemagne. An overdecorated table, absent smiles that are harder to stomach than their absence. That's the way it goes: each Christmas Eve brings its own bitter flavour. It occurred to me that had the Virgin Mary had an abortion, we could have gone to the cinema... Hélène is sombre, tense. She is distancing herself. I've stopped trying to keep hold. The children have to grin and bear it, killing time until New Year's Eve: a night belonging only to them and from which we are excluded without question.

That year, Hélène decided not to stay in Nice. Attached as she is to this house that watched her grow, after two days, the cord that binds them starts to fray. Out of routine habit (and habit is a friend to the lazy), it has become the site of family gatherings. A family of four. I never knew Hélène's parents and she didn't know mine. We were both orphans; I was much older than her – everything was still to be discovered. We invented exemplary mothers and textbook fathers for ourselves. But family legend is no match for the test of matrimony. A few years after our wedding, our parents went back to seeming just like everyone else's: fragile, imperfect, unjust; for some alcoholics, for others cheats and cowards.

My confessions gave Hélène the upper hand. She would tell anyone who'd listen:

'The apple doesn't fall far from the tree!'

I'm not really cheating on her any more. At least, not in a serious way. One or two (three?) recent but meaningless affairs. I'm not what you'd call a chaser. Too anxious for it. Seducing, sometimes loving, is reassuring. But when I sleep with a woman, it's me I'm making love to. I expect to be thanked. If she's upset, I go in cold. After orgasm, I don't take her in my arms. I put my watch back on, hail a taxi, promise that next time we'll have more time. Truth be told, there was one in particular who made her mark on me. If I made her promises in the dead of night, when I went home in the morning, I felt for Hélène and her coloured lines, her doubts, her fragility, even her aggressiveness, a tenderness that erased all promises I'd made to the other. Then came the ultimatum: my mistress was in love and refused to live her life on the sidelines. I bought myself time by lavishing gifts and making promises. At first she indulged me, saying she was prepared to wait. Then one day, out of the blue, I was busy stroking her softly, waiting for the customary token sigh of satisfaction, when suddenly she pulled away, handed me my watch and left. She never replied to my messages again. I'd been unhappy, unfair to Hélène. Now I was relieved to be rid of this affair.

Hélène understood I needed to go through this. We never spoke about it. It was around that time her painted landscapes and faces became less sharp, more abstract.

Sometimes I visit call-girls. I ask how much, come quickly, put my watch back on, hand over the money. Never a penny more. I turn up my collar and head into town, nameless and unhappy.

For the first time in a long time, I decided to take a few days to make the most of the winter sun before heading back to Paris.

Because it is December 25th, and because a date has a way of bringing its ancestors to mind, I think about that strange bird wrapped up in an oversized coat I met on Christmas day long ago.

I remember that young girl, melancholy, stooped. Lost and far from where she was sitting.

I still don't know what made me sit down beside her. I felt as if I'd been guided by a steady hand, as if it would be unnatural not to join her. More than anything, I didn't have a choice.

This girl was younger than my own children today. She was surrounded by a moat, like a castle with its drawbridge raised.

I wasn't attracted to her. But instinct told me she was in danger, that it fell to me (Why? How?) to protect, warm and guide her. Without knowing her, I recognised her.

After minutes spent watching, she was now part of me. What body was hidden under that heavy coat with its gigantic buttons? I didn't plan our first contact. I had no strategy. I wasn't looking to seduce her. The age difference between us ruled out anything other than a kind hello.

What to do with this weary, wandering elf?

This was over thirty years ago. I remember asking her: 'Jeanne, can we see each other again?'

'Yes.'

'Here, this afternoon?'

'I'll be here.'

# Jeanne

I have to get back to the hotel – my mother is waiting. I met a man who suggested we meet at the same place later that afternoon. We exchanged only first names. He could almost be my father.

She is snoozing, *Volodya* on her lap. Her perfume is all over the room. I kiss her softly and stroke a patch of her brand-new hair, a little tuft sprouting eagerly, unaware it will never live to be a curl or a plait. I look at it, day after day, amazed at this persistence of life that will not give up, in spite of everything, standing tall amid the ruins and abandoned bodies. I grab a pencil. The memory of Gabriel's face starts to emerge on a page torn from my sketchbook.

She is waking up, in pain, I know it.

'Where were you?'

'In a park, not far.'

'Did you sleep well?'

'What about you, mum, did you sleep well?'

'Oh, you know me, as soon as I wake it's party time!'

Struggling to sit up, she suggests we go for breakfast in the hotel restaurant.

She does her best to hide the pain brought on by simple acts like getting out of bed. In the lift, she looks at herself in the mirror, staring but not managing to reconcile this grimace of a smile with the beauty she once was. She is searching for one but finds the other. She has only three floors to convince herself that, no – she doesn't know this frightening form. She tilts her head back to set her long, vanished hair back in place.

Walking slowly, determined to make the most of the time, we arrive at the restaurant decorated with rotating carousels. Endlessly turning, there is one horse, in particular, with holes in its hair where the paint on its mane has worn away. My mother leans in: 'Hello there son! Looks as if I'm not the only one thinning up top!'

The waiter hands us massive menus. We each disappear behind our own, giving us both space to breathe, time to relax our faces. Hers is tight with pain. Then she pulls a little jewellery box from her bag and says: 'Merry Christmas my darling!'

In this moment, she is the child gifting its parent, waiting for a reaction. She is watching me. I open the box. Inside, a ring. Three pretty stones that seem to be levitating.

'I saw this and thought to myself: this ring is for you. The stones look as if they are propping themselves up. One day, you too will have to prop yourself up. At first it will be hard, very hard. You'll feel as if you've forgotten how to walk and talk. Early on, you'll be paralysed. One foot in front of the other, you'll walk to Pont-Neuf. Then, little by little, you'll walk further, for longer: la Rue de Buci, Saint-Sulpice, la Rue du Regard. And back. These will be your achievements. You'll have to learn to be Jeanne without a mother. Learn too not to say that word, "mum". So silly – a single syllable, so available. It will be forbidden, just like that, in less time than it takes to die. You'll have to learn a new alphabet. You'll realise that when you use the old one, people no longer understand you. To those you've loved and who've loved you, you'll be nothing more than Jeanne who has lost her mother. Mourning will be your core. Impossible to hide. I know full well you'll learn. But you'll want to give up; you'll wander off track. You won't recognise your apartment building, your street, the neighbourhood. You'll make new friends that will know me only as the past. They'll each picture me their own way: my voice, my smile, based entirely on your memories. You see, when words and courage fail you, you will look at these small stones supporting themselves.'

In this moment we too are hanging in mid-air. We have to hold onto what remains of life. We have to pretend. The food is good. Every now and then she dozes off, as if sampling death. She isn't present. Now it's my turn to give her a gift: a blue flecked woollen jumper with a gigantic Tintin embroidered on it, his dog Snowy in tow.

'It's wonderful! I love it. Help me put it on!'

I didn't tell her that I'd met a man in the park that morning.

Before going back to her room, she browses the gift shop in the lobby. She is determined to buy a cap, tee shirt or scarf with the hotel's name on it. She rakes through items meant for tourists, even though she is a native. A native of this light; a light that promises clear nights. Still, she wants a souvenir from our trip, and settles on a cap she uses immediately to cover her head. She is used to hiding her baldness. I take it off her gently and tell her there is no need to hide from now on.

I take her back to her room. She climbs on the bed, wedges herself between the pillows, and asks for a shawl to wrap herself in. I leave the door between our rooms ajar. I want to watch over her afternoon sleep. It's a cunning sort, this one: it seems to promise rest, but this nap – I can tell – is one she may not survive. Still, she doesn't want me to sit beside her, waiting for her to wake, to fall asleep, for the pain to subside. She tells me to go and burn a candle for Rita, patron Saint of lost causes (it's thanks to her she passed her school exams, she used to say).

'Tell her to do something about *the ache...*'

This is what she calls the bone cancer that is killing her slowly, like a torturer.

I pause for a moment in my grandmother's room. She too has a gift for me.

'Come in, my treasure! Come closer. I'm going to give you something very precious: a keepsake you'll give to your children who will then pass it on to their children.'

I sit on the floor in a corner of the room and listen as she hums:

*'Tumbala, Tumbala, Tumbalalaika*
*Tumbala, Tumbala, Tumbalalaika*
*Tumbalalaika, shpil balalaika*
*Tumbalalaika freylekh zol zayn.'*

I close my eyes. I picture her as a little girl, her hands tapping to the beat of her mother's rhyme.

'You know, Olga, Freiga, and me, we used to dance in a circle to the tune. The house was calm. Mama was sitting beside the samovar. Life was sweet, peaceful.

Then one day, my father came in yelling: "Hurry, grab what you can, they are charging into homes on horseback and burning them!"

My sisters and me, we were so afraid we forgot to cry. We put the candelabrum and the clock in the cart. Mama wrapped the breadknife in a cloth. She took Freiga, the littlest, and hid her among our things. Papa took care of the horses. We escaped the massacre. And so began a life of wandering. We walked for months, maybe years. I don't know anymore. But we were alive, together. Lev and Meyer were born in Paris. Papa swore an oath to France – the country that welcomed us. So you understand, this tune must be passed down. It has followed us everywhere, Olga, Freiga, and me, and we've never stopped dancing. My father went on praying every Friday night for the Tsar that chased us away. And as for hatred, my mother banished it breastfeeding Lev and Meyer. We were alive; we still are. Go, my treasure, and meet Gabriel. Go my love, go and live.'

'How do you know about Gabriel?'

'I am in all moments at once. Only the living experience

time as fragmented.'

I kissed her. As I closed the door, I heard her humming the tune she had just passed down to me. I swear I could make out sounds of other voices joining her, all three blending in harmony.

I will remember that melody. It will be my way of putting her in a cart and carrying her across the coming century. My children will learn it and sing it to their children.

I put on my armour, my red woolly hat, a cross between Cousteau and a comic cartoon character.

I set off for the park, wearing the pretty ring with its self-supporting stones, my grandmother's whispers in Yiddish over my shoulder.

# Gabriel

The house is empty. The Christmas tree seems to have wilted in a few hours. For lunch, a slice of yesterday's yule log will do.

Hélène rings to say she has arrived safely. Even if monotone, her voice was comforting. Earlier I had found her annoying, infuriating even. Gentle Hélène, who has spent her whole life tuning out her own needs, is now kicking up a storm.

Our life as we'd known it hadn't vanished exactly, rather it had been disguised, yet so unconvincingly I could still recognise its outlines, even if returning there was becoming an impossibility.

I no longer recognise the house. Still, its furniture and smell are familiar; a perfume of memory hangs in the air that lingers and sticks to me.

I'm wide awake; I can't sleep. My skin is crawling. Many voices echo. I realise these are my own, calling for attention. The one belonging to the child in the playground drowns out the shy teenager. The voice belonging to the Law student merges with the married man. I hear the difference between my fatherly tone and the sounds of the Parisian lawyer I've become. These voices are burrowing a tunnel to escape; my only hope of finding peace lies in establishing harmony between them. It's as if I'm listening to an orchestra warming up for a performance, waiting for that moment in which the brass and string sections finally come together. It is the whole that gives value to each separate element.

These inner voices bring me comfort; I relax. The little boy asks the lawyer: 'Do you know how to play Jacks?'

The adult sighs, crouches, and sits down in his suit. His jacket is restricting his movements, so he takes it off. Puts on his glasses because his vision is poor. The younger of the two scoops up the pieces in a confident sweep. The adult smiles, admiring the child's fearlessness.

Now the teenager turns boastfully to the seated man and tells him there's no way he's going to end up looking like *that*... He'll make his own world without rules. Looks him up and down, dismisses him. The adult smiles knowingly.

I wake two hours later from a pitch-black sleep. Every sleep has its colours and shapes. This time it was a dense circle.

Again, I was determined to either silence these voices, or force them to hear one another.

Between this morning and now, I've lived not a life but the promise of one. I remembered this precise encounter, this tiny silhouette engulfed by unbearable grief.

Jeanne looked unlike anyone I'd ever met. She was more intriguing than enticing; it wasn't sexual attraction that drew me in. She could have been my daughter... Actually, no: she could never have been; it would have pained me to have such a sad-looking child, wide-eyed, cowering behind a distant smile. My daughter would have been accessible, open.

Life had deserted this bird. We had only just said goodbye, but I kept her in my sights for a while. Her earphones looked like extensions of her head. She seemed indifferent to everything. Having just found her, I knew I couldn't lose this. She had reached an untouched part of me.

I left the park and went home. Or rather, back to Blanche's house. Blanche was a childless aunt of mine (through marriage) who had come to think of me as her son. Most of the time she merely tolerated me, but there were times I could feel she loved me. Her memory was fading. She called me Gabriel or Justin, using my name or my father's, yet I never paid attention to the label I'd been given. Perhaps I was already too cynical. All that mattered was her house: a true haven. On the occasions she mistook me for my father, I caught her tender words in mid-air, never gladly, yet still gratefully, because after all, she put a roof over my head. Blanche passed away after a good innings, refusing to the bitter end to admit she was over ninety. As she made no last will and testament, she left her house to me by default. At the burial, one or two very old ladies came over to me, probing together: 'You must be Justin?'

When I met Jeanne, I was looking after this house all by myself. I hardly ever came here. As there was nothing waiting for me in Nice, I had been intending to sell it...

I pick up a few shreds of wrapping paper and throw them on the firewood as kindling for later. I'm going to lie down on the green velvet sofa in the living room. I need to sleep. When I wake up I'll have forgotten Jeanne, Blanche, this house belonging to me without ever being mine. It was over thirty years ago.

Jeanne... When I wake the memory rushes back. I remember being late for our first meeting. She was waiting for me on a bench, wrapped up in her coat.

# *The afternoon*

## Jeanne

Locating Saint Rita's chapel is a matter of life or death. Crossing the flower-market, I head towards Old Town.

I'm guided to it. I'm there. The church is quite big. I look for Saint Rita, but Christ on the cross has stolen the limelight. Given the fact the church bears her name, I'd assumed she would be its heroine. By the entrance, to the left, I find an icon of the saint surrounded by a wall of red candles. Tiny, set against a blue backdrop, she seems to be floating, gentle and graceful.

I buy a candle I light with a long match that is ready and waiting on the table. Soon, one of these flames will serve as both beacon and witness.

I have no idea how to talk to an image. We look at each other. I daren't be the first to speak. So I count the candles while I pluck up the courage.

Then I go for it.

'I'm here for my mother. She always said she passed her school exams thanks to you, Saint of lost causes. And here you are, floating between two suns, looking as if you don't really care. But it isn't a philosophy test I need help with today. I'm not here to ask for tips on a history or geography exam, or for favours in maths. This is serious. Do you hear me? Actually, I don't think you hear anything... All you care about is lining up as many little lights as possible by your feet like a plane landing on a runway. But listen – that's my opinion, and this isn't about me. I'm here to deliver a message from my mother: she wants to get well. Do you understand? Get well. If enduring torture is a prerequisite for sainthood, I promise you she's served her time. Do you know how it feels to run your hand over a memory? The memory of a breast, of a happy moment? What it's like to wake up screaming? To tear yourself in two just by turning over in bed? To be locked out of your own child's future? To have exhausted all treatments, even ones not yet officially available, to have worked your way through all doctors, from the most competent to the charmers and charlatans? To know that the baby brought into the world by your own daughter will be rocked to sleep by another grandmother? Well – haven't you anything to say? When I get back to the hotel, what will I tell my mother? I'll lie to her. Like the doctors and her friends, both real and fake. Don't worry mum: I saw Saint Rita in her sunlit sky and she's taking care of you. I'll say she must stick at the chemo, but I'll tell her you are having a word with Him upstairs. After all, you do have friends in high places!

Still, you say nothing. Even your candle flames have stopped moving. You don't often see flames as still as this. I guess too much indifference snuffs out even the brightest lights. I came to see you because a woman's light is fading. Yes, fading. Just like one of your candles. But when they go out, it's because they've reached the end of their life. No wax, no life. Then a replacement candle uses the base of its melted predecessor to fix itself to the spot. My mother isn't done with her life. She made a good start, but was stopped in her tracks.

I'll tell her you listened to me, that I read the messages in the little book illuminated by the flames of the grateful who have lit candles and prayed in your name. I think I'll even tell her you smiled at me, Saint Rita.'

A pen is tied to the book with a piece of string coiling in spirals. Below a message I assume is written in Russian, I jot down:

*Dear Saint Rita,*

*Thank you for everything. Thank you for your silence, thank you for your indifference, thank you for those who have hoped right up to the final moment. Thank you for the hair, thank you for the breast. Thank you for screwing her life.*

*Jeanne.*

*P.S. If you see my father, tell him to shave because his wife is coming.*

Gabriel isn't at the meeting point. I'm disappointed. How can you be disappointed by someone you hardly know? Never mind. At least I got some air. And I do need air. I'm living this agony day in day out. Watching my mother deteriorate, powerless to relieve her, I'm like a scanner measuring the speed of decline. But I can be there for her. Laugh and make promises. Tell her about Jacques: the Parisian I've fallen for. Tell her odd things about our affair (but leave out the part where he described my looks as underwhelming...) As I invent stories, I create a man. I repeat words he never said to me. I pretend he is reassuring and generous. I tell my mother, eager to hear about his qualities, that I can count on him. I dream up a future from which she is excluded. I curate my own faith, drawing from all I've learned as a painter. I tell her that, little by little, I want to abandon the symbolic, to hint at things, to infer, to suggest. I want to do away with universal symbols and one day create my own alphabet, my codes. Access is open to all who want to enter.

She listens to me, knowing she will never see my landscapes or portraits beyond the recent run-of-the-mill pieces; she hasn't the time to witness any evolution in my work. My early-career inexperience will be forever fixed in her eternity.

So yes, I'm happy for a few hours' rest.

'Jeanne?'

'Hello Gabriel.'

'I'm sorry I'm late. You look freezing. Can I buy you some tea, a glass of wine, a hot chocolate, a crepe, a waffle?'

'All these things!'

We stepped into a brasserie, a warm haven for survivors of the morning's festivities.

'Are you alone in Nice?'

'No – I'm with my mother and grandmother. And you?'

'I used to come here every year at Christmas to visit my aunt. Then two years ago I inherited her house, even though she couldn't remember my first name and was convinced I was her father. So I keep coming at Christmas, alone, to this town and big house that's seen and heard everything. There's no escaping it! And you, Jeanne?'

'My mother is very ill. She wanted to come back to her birthplace. And my grandmother has come along too.'

We talk for a while. He asks me about my studies, so I tell him about my love of painting, how – for want of talent – I'm very driven. I'm talking rubbish, without reason, without logic. I jump from cancer to Ukraine without attempting coherence. I give myself over to him, my tears filled with words.

Gabriel doesn't interrupt me; he pours me tea, makes me drink to warm up. Even suggests I take off my red hat.

'And your father?'

'My father let me down. I adored him, but he died.'

My father comes back to me, his voice, his look, his determination, his battles.

'He took over the family printing company after the war. He was the only Holocaust survivor in his generation. Lev and Meyer, my grandmother's brothers, had built a successful business. But they never came back from hell.'

I tell him more and more. I hear my grandmother's

44

voice humming the tune, and picture Lev and Meyer cradled, being breastfed by their mother who is whispering thanks to God and to France for having saved them.

I recall my father's anxiety when he was first told about his wife's illness. I describe his death: dry, simple, disgusting. A death we both denied, mother and daughter. Yet it was actually during the most violent moments of denial that we grew closest.

That clinical question: "Why him?" got the better of my spirit, my budding femininity. A little girl, a fresh half-orphan, I used to wonder: where are my tears? My secret pain was a mystery to the adults around me who were clueless about child suffering.

'As I drink this tea now, I could swear he's alive. As alive as you, Gabriel, sitting there. As alive as me. And so much more alive than my dying mother.'

'How did your father die?'

'He committed suicide.'

'Suicide... How?'

'Hanged himself, just like that.'

'Just like that?'

'Yes... He always did enjoy immediate pleasures without thinking about the consequences.'

I talk to him as if I've known him forever. Yet if I seem coy and candid in equal measure, it's precisely because I do not know him.

'I'm eight years old; my mother is ill. She locks herself in the bathroom. Terrified, through the gap in the door I hear her vomiting. I'm ten; she is losing her hair for the first time. I look at her pillow when I get home from school. In the dark, it looks like blood. But no. There are no open wounds with this illness. Everything is insidious, hidden. I'm thirteen; she is doing better. Her hair has grown back. I'm fifteen when one evening she tells me they are going to remove a breast. I'm sixteen; her hair falls out again. She wants me to go with her to buy a wig. In the shop I hear the overwhelmed shopkeeper advise she go blonde on Mondays, redhead on Wednesdays, then brunette on weekends. I'm seventeen when she shows me her tattoo: "It's for the rays. Look! Don't you think I look like a tribal chief? Go and buy me a wig with two plaits!" I'm twenty when we celebrate a year of remission. We will never celebrate two. Since then, the illness has come back, stronger. The chemo, the hair, the rays, the chemo, the hair, the rays – a round dance from which there is no escape.'

I tell him all this, all in one breath, without stopping.

Gabriel takes his turn and speaks softly. Tells me about himself, the wife he will meet one day, the children they will have, the good life they will make for themselves. I find it strange he isn't already married. He smiles at me and asks does he look old enough to be? He tells me about his job. Talks about the blind trust clients place in him. The belief justice will be served. Tells me that in courtrooms which are mostly open to the public, the hopes of the victim or the person on trial must take a seat in the audience. In this theatre, the letter of the law is worshipped and raw suffering is met with protocol. The whole set-up, he tells me, is designed to protect, not to please; the upside to wearing gowns is they make all actors appear equal, creating a sort of mock objectivity free from material considerations. Embellishments on gowns should be forbidden, he says, because some colleagues wear so many military medals they end up looking like Field Marshals in the courtroom. He campaigns for the word – the only tool available to the prosecution or defence – as the only element worthy of judge or jury consideration. I study him, more and more closely, ever more intensely. His voice, his look, his gestures.

He orders himself another glass of white wine. I stick to tea.

I look at my watch, panicked, carried away by time that's been playing dead. Even if powerless to heal, Gabriel's voice has soothed me. It's time to end the truce, time to get back in line. Cancer has come to collect me, so I take its hand, and together we walk back to the hotel.

But before we part ways, Gabriel asks me: 'Do you want to come to the house tonight?'

I said yes. Yes, of course. Gabriel is drawing me in. I'm being careless; I don't know him. But there's a sense of certainty to my intuition: after this meeting, I will be someone else. A Jeanne unknown to me, asking for the chance to be heard.

He gives me his address, and I put on my hat, button my coat and put away my little white sketchbook that has been tainted by Gabriel's eyes, his smile.

I put in my earphones so I can lose myself in the sound of Yves Montand. We leave the café together. He doesn't offer to take me back to the hotel. We say goodbye, each looking forward already to our next meeting. Night has fallen, but the palms are lit up. I look to the sea and I sing:

*'When a soldier leaves for war, he takes in a bag his baton for marching, when a soldier returns from the war, he brings in his bag his clothes for starching.'*

In this moment, I am that soldier. My baton is the promise of a peaceful and cancer-free life. The promise of this white house whose walls won't have to witness any more tragedy. My baton stands for those teenage years and the demons yet to catch up with me.

In my bag there is cancer, a wig tucked between pairs of shoes, a prosthetic breast tossed on the bed between pillows, two bottles of wine, sorry they were emptied so unceremoniously. Also in my bag: my father's death, my mother's screams. But above all, my silence. No tears, no shouting. A heartache phantom who won't take off his mask until he's undercover and safely out of sight. One day, I'm going to have to talk about this silence. I'm a soldier too – I've been at war. At war with reality, denying my father's absence at every turn, now my mother's agony. And Gabriel guided me to a trench to take shelter for a few hours. Still, I had to dig for myself, even if there were two of us. Hacking away, for a long time, I gave way to the truth. It isn't a life I've been creating, rather people to live in it.

On this day, December 25th, Gabriel handed me the pickaxe – proof he was ready to go with me down into the depths.

# Gabriel

I left Jeanne behind, happy for this moment. Touched deeply by her frailty, I watched as she walked away in her red hat, her sketched outline gradually fading.

We had spent almost three hours together. It was as though we recognised ourselves in each other. She told me her life story, all too quickly, as if crossing the entire world in one night. We were strangers to the future, burying hopes born out of love for a few glasses of wine and a fallen tear.

Her voice so earnest I couldn't help but smile, Jeanne told me she was a painter; painting was all she knew. She'd have liked to take over the family printing business and learn to read the Cyrillic and Hebraic alphabets, but above all she wanted to write. To put colours on words, to create material by linking sentences, giving meaning to the whole, to describe her feelings instead of merely representing them. Words, she told me, far outnumber the spectrum's colours, even if she didn't imagine for one second she had discovered them all. She wanted to compile a dictionary of synonyms listing all possible colour equivalents instead of replacement words.

When she refused to show me the contents of her sketchbook, I didn't insist. She was disappointed.

I wanted to cradle her in my arms.

She told me her father was a printer and editor, which in turn led her to ask about my job. She seemed intrigued, so I told her about this complicated and horrendous case I'd been working on where one of my less esteemed colleagues had taken advantage of a vulnerable man who had misplaced his trust in him, believing that if he signed the proposed document on the dotted line, and marked each page with his initials, his life would go back to normal. It did not.

I told her about my early days as a court-appointed

junior lawyer, quick hearings during which I defended clients to the best of my ability, without even having the chance to hear their voices. She played with the sugar wrappers as she listened, dividing them into small squares with her fingernail, then folding them to make tiny boats. By the time we had finished our tea and white wine, she had built herself an entire fleet and lined them up, side by side, each ready to defend its partner.

Impressed, I praised the armada.

'Well, I am at war,' she said.

'In that case, you should bore tiny holes in the hull for canons. Battles aren't won with optimism alone!'

I didn't take her hand; she offered it to me. I listened carefully to the story of her father's apparent suicide without giving much context. In truth, it sounded as if a heart attack had killed him. Clearly this red-hatted sparrow with ice-cold hands had spent too long clutching at death.

In a few hours, Jeanne had guided me through her world of ghosts and rebellion.

I felt as if I'd been drafted into a mission: it was my duty to restore her father to his rightful place by entertaining Jeanne's fantasies, bringing him back to life so that she might finally let him go.

Why do memories come flooding back? Hélène had only just left, and yet there I was: moved by the mere glimpse of Jeanne's fragility, merciless and violent.

Hélène is now beyond reach; she hears only the children and their demands. For them, she was as ever-present as I've been absent. As she entered motherhood, gradually she shied away from my look, my touch, my longing. She was calm on the day she told me she could no longer live two lives in one. Whenever our vampiric children granted her a moment's peace, hesitantly she would get out her easel and paintbrushes. Eventually, she started painting again. Her children and house in the countryside were her only sources of inspiration. I encouraged her out of kindness, even if Hélène knew she had no talent. Maybe there was sometimes the odd glimpse of something special, but it was rare. I watched, without ever admitting it, as she broke away from the very reality she aimed to reproduce. She wanted a geometrical form to contain a world. In a talk she once gave, she told a packed auditorium that the only person who required talent was the onlooker; a painter, she claimed, can only gesture to a viewer's genius. I never contradicted her, even if I was concerned about the increasingly abstract nature of her pieces.

My career took off. Absent-mindedly I skimmed defence cases that my co-counsel (who were terrified of upsetting me) would read and digest on my behalf, summarising the issues and jurisdictions. Then I would plead a client's defence, often winning. On my gown, the odd decoration added some colour.

# Jeanne

On my way back to the hotel, Reggiani started playing straight after Yves Montand. Night had fallen. To my own surprise I realise I'd hardly thought about my mother during the time alone with Gabriel.

I'm with her no matter what happens. I want to believe I'm strong enough to win this fight for her. Yet often, all too often, I catch myself hoping this nightmare will end quickly, very quickly, before I fall ill myself. I know full well it isn't contagious, and yet here we are: both dying from it.

The sea, the palms, the Promenade des Anglais. For almost a year now everything around me has seemed to be pulling away. A tree moves me, a guitar solo blows me away.

I hurry back, practically running. What state will I find her in? Asleep? Alive? Unconscious? So many questions whirling around for so long now, every time I leave her.

She is stretched out, asleep. Her glasses have slid down past the bridge of her nose. The book is open at a page far from her bookmark. Her lips are the colour of her skin. She is wearing jeans and a pink linen blouse. Around her neck, the ivory chain my father gave her. I won't wake her. When she opens her eyes, she will find on her bedside table a palm tree arching over a turquoise sea, both lit by a red sun (I'd run out of yellow paint!)

I'm going to dive in the golden tub and swim a few lengths.

I think about Gabriel. What is it he wants? He is attractive, he intrigues me. I want, so badly, to talk to him again. When he listens to me, my feelings and memories pass through a filter that makes them feel weightless. Heartache's corners are rounded, and even if the waves of pain are still intense, they aren't as long-lasting. For the time I spend

53

talking to him, they are fixed here, in this café in Nice.

While our meeting lasted, there was the sea in Paris.

But I want something else. That same morning, I didn't know he existed, and yet I already feel his authority, attentiveness, determination, tenderness. Just now I was looking at his hands, picturing his index finger with a ring fixed tightly to it. Then quickly it will shrink. Later the skin will crown the ring, not the other way around. While he spoke, I imagined taking off this ring he isn't yet wearing and playing with it. Of course, he doesn't see me doing this, but I try it on my finger that is too slim to hold it. I like the gap between his ring and my other fingers; I'm like a little girl pretending she has married her father.

I find my grandmother still sitting in the armchair where I'd left her a few hours earlier, mid-conversation. She doesn't see me. I'm a ghost. She isn't smiling; she is agitated. She is speaking to someone, but I can't make out who it is. I don't want to disturb her, so I withdraw, then she shouts:

'Enough! You must let her come with us! These gherkins will only last three more days and I've already run out of buckwheat.'

In the darkness, her silver candelabrum guides me to where she is. I want to kiss her and tell her that all day long I've been humming the tune from earlier. But I feel her face pull back from my kiss. Her pearls are still floating free, hanging on a memory of skin. I sit down on the floor, eyes fixed on the clock's golden hands. My grandmother has gone quiet. In this silence, a lost world, I know. In this silence, Olga, Freiga, Meyer, and Lev are no longer singing. In this silence, I hear *The Kaddish*, the prayer for the dead, rising up. In this silence, the death of her only son. I promise my grandmother, as if talking to myself, I'll be happy. Right now I want to immortalise her in my sketchbook. My drawing captures her, here, in this old hotel room in Nice. I tear out the page and hand her the portrait. She thanks me, smiling.

Yet, on the page, all I see is an empty armchair in the darkness in a room that looks cursed. I put it down on the small table.

'Jeanne? Are you there?'
'Yes! In my bathtub.'

My mother is awake. I wasn't worried because I recognised this sort of sleep: the ceasefire kind that interrupts the pain. From across their opposing lines, soldiers had called a truce, gathering strength from the memories of their former lives. Lost in her own world, my mother remembers herself looking pretty and whole with a thick mass of hair, a loose, lengthy skirt and espadrilles with laces that creep up her ankles. A shirt tied around her waist and a shoulder bag. It's summer and she's in Nice. Colette and Michel are in the car honking the horn. Tonight there's a party at Marie-France's place. She is so pretty, my mother. She clings to this dream to make the respite last.

For its part, cancer respects the rule. It looks back over all the people it has taken prisoner, some executed, others spared. A breast held hostage without even a hope of ransom. This hair loss is a spoil of war. It will win – there is no doubt. For the moment, it is savouring its most recent victories. On chemo days it keeps a low profile, retreats. But it's all the better to eat you with, my dear.

Waking up is a signal to attack; pain's foot-soldiers start their advance. My mother fights back with pills and mouthfuls of red wine. We make use of the weapons we have; the certainty of outcome doesn't stop us resisting. She doesn't cry. She never cries in front of me.

'I know the docs are lying. They can't face telling me I'm dying. But it isn't that hard. It's not exactly complicated! Or maybe it is. They talk about hope, some new treatment on the horizon that hasn't even been developed yet. This so-called cure is a figment of their imagination, I know it is. This bloody cancer, it caught me twenty years too early. There's nothing they can do for me. They are watching me destroy myself, but don't try to stop me. They even offer me cigarettes to go with my glass of wine! They are in league with the devil. They thrive off this illness. No cancer, no cigar. My death cements their power. They are phonies, last-minute resistants, collaborators saying they wish they'd seen the light. They tread on my hair, my breasts, my future, things I long for but I'll never have again!'

She is distressed, powerless, angry.

'What did you do this afternoon?' she asks.

'I went walking in Old Town.'

'Did you see Saint Rita?'

'Course I did! We talked, and all I can say is you have a powerful ally there!'

I told her about the candles and the stone ex-votos. I even invented a queue. I told my dying mother that Saint Rita smiled at me, set against her backdrop of suns, that she reached out to me kindly, even warmly.

A lifelong atheist and sceptic, my mother listens to me, smiling like a satisfied child who has just realised that the glass of milk and biscuits left for Santa Claus have disappeared. So I continue talking.

'You know, I read the messages left in the book just beside the donation box… and Saint Rita has cured people who are far more ill than you.'

I hadn't read anything of the sort; I'd only skimmed the words. My mother smiled: a smile I hadn't seen in a long time, one of hope.

She said she was too tired to eat out.

'How about some champagne and room service?'

'I'd love to!'

We read the menu together: smoked salmon, tomato salad, Bollinger.

'Perfect,' she said.

I remember thinking my grandmother's gherkins would make a nice addition.

# Gabriel

On my way home after leaving Jeanne, I passed by the church that is home to Saint Rita's chapel. For the first time ever, I pushed open the door. On the left, a portrait of the saint and flickering candles. Perhaps because it was December 25th – or maybe this saint works miracles all year round? – I lit a candle. I thought long and hard about the wording of my wish. What to ask for on Jeanne's behalf? That she make a living off painting? That she realise sometimes hard work can make up for talent? That her mother might either recover, or die, but either way, for a swift end to it all? That she forgive her father for leaving her? And the unhappy ones who have deserted her, her mother, both of them? And as for me, what do I wish for? To see her again. To understand her. To offer wisdom. To protect her. Every wish I made was for her. The candle wick starts burning. What was he really wishing for – this loner whose inner flame sparked in the very moment he struck the match? A child's healing? A rekindled love? Trust restored? Peace in death? A past-tense illness? An end to war somewhere, a conflict's delayed outcome?

Then I notice a small book lit up by the candles. I skim through, stopping at the word 'Jeanne'. I read the line above it: *Thank you for screwing her life.*

A coincidence? It must be. There is more than one Jeanne in the world. I glanced for the last time at Saint Rita, then at the candle I'd just lit.

All I thought about was Jeanne. My need for her was becoming urgent, wild. It wasn't tenderness she was calling for just then. I had no intention of becoming her instructor, a new teacher, yet I wanted to feel her in my grasp. I wanted to fulfil her, to help her stem the tide, even when I'm no longer around. Forming a part of her might just be my life's purpose from now on.

The house was deserted. Even Blanche's shadow had taken leave, gone to haunt the neighbours. Waiting for Jeanne, I wondered: why was this young girl coming over? We had nothing in common. She must be at least twenty years my junior.

I put a bottle of white wine in the fridge and tidied the living room.

The waiting began - a wait like a dreamless snooze. My mind was empty. I had no plan. A painful wait. Hadn't she just criticised me for mistaking lust for love, my single motivation the need for the release of a quick and fierce ejaculation? It was just then, in that moment, it dawned on me what I'd really been feeling. I wanted not to hear it, but there's no escaping your own inner voice. Raw and unchecked, it cried out that I'd never known love, how to make up half of a whole. Pelted with judgements, I want to defend myself, find explanations, but none come. I'm guilty.

This is a living memory: candles, waiting, the promise of pleasure. I'm older now. I've kept myself in check, justified the injustices witnessed on a daily basis, all to mask the bitterness. Thirty years after my first meeting with Jeanne, I'm still haunted by the jolting awareness that I, alone, was the cause of Hélène's unhappiness. I am judged for having deserted my wife, body and soul.

That voice is still screaming: 'What about Hélène? You stopped caressing her, touching her, kissing her. Eventually, you even stopped looking at her, talking to her. She became a convenient companion, a pet, meek and mild. Did she expire? Become outdated?'

I say nothing. It's my turn to sit in the dock.

# *The evening*

## Jeanne

Dinner has arrived. My mother is wearing make-up: blusher on her cheeks, lip gloss and mascara. I'm her date for the night. I don't want to disappoint her, so I swap my grey tee shirt for another: this one has a token Mickey printed on it. I spray her perfume so I can carry her around everywhere with me. She wants to eat everything, but doesn't dare touch anything. I try forcing her: 'Make an effort!'

'I can't! My mouth is burning, my stomach is burning, my back is burning.'

I suggest we make her a Biafine dessert. She laughs and I watch as the colour returns to her cheeks beneath her foundation.

'What are we doing here?' she asks me. 'What the hell are we doing in this hotel? I wanted to come to Nice to see the palms and the sea, but apart from Colette's living room, all I've seen of the skyline is the lift, restaurant and gift shop. I need air – I'm suffocating. This disease is eating away at me inside. I'm done for. I know I'm done for. And you, don't tell me you don't know it! Everyone knows it. You are all waiting for me to die, right here and now. There's no end to this agony! And what about you, my poor Jeanne? A life filled with scanners, chemo, radiation. Look at you! You have no clue how to grow up. Just look at you. You'll never be a woman with a mother like me. You're twenty-five but you look thirteen! Are you sure he's real, this guy in Paris? I can't imagine who'd be interested in you, daughter of cancer and a heart attack. I can feel this beast taking a leisurely stroll inside my body. Wandering, it wants a bone, a liver, a lung, then the rest… Or maybe not the lung, the stomach instead, or why not both! They are all on the menu. It's an open bar.

How will you manage, after this? Who will love you? Who will spoil you? Who is going to listen to you? Who will believe you? Who will wait for you to come home? Tomorrow comes soon, Jeanne. What the hell am I doing here in this hotel? I was born in Nice, but I don't want to die here. I don't want to die, full stop. Do you hear, Jeanne? You want to know what drives me crazy? Knowing I won't see you any more. I won't hear your voice. And my grandchildren... I won't look after them when their parents go out. They won't have their own bedroom in my house. You know, the Tuesday-night bedroom, the Saturday bedroom. I won't pick them up from school, won't buy for them the things they need. What kind of woman are you going to be, Jeanne? Who is the man that will give you his name? What will you call your children? What kind of mother will you be? Who will comfort you when you are down? I'm tired, so tired. Pour me another glass of champagne. And fetch my pills. See, it isn't me that's crying – it's the grandmother I'll never be. It's stupid, I know. My grandchildren, you'll have to love them for us both. Enough for you and for me. You will tell them about me. Tell them I'd have loved them more than life itself. And you'll take them to New York, ice-skating in Central Park, and feed bread to the pigeons in St Mark's square. You'll introduce them to Mozart and Jacques Demy. You'll open accounts for them at the library so they can take out books and whatever else. But above all you'll tell them that from non-existent Paradise, most likely from hell, or from dull purgatory, I'm watching over them... Ah, some champagne – thank you. See, I just said "champagne" in the same way they say "The End". And that's a wrap!'

I let her talk without interrupting, her speech slowed by the mix of alcohol and medications. I have no voice, no words, no arms and legs left to move. Mickey is sobbing across my tee shirt.

She staggers as she stands up. I help her take off her make-up and put on her pyjamas. I prop her up until she reaches the bed, then arrange the pillows so that she feels supported and tucked in. There's an art to it. She wants her book, a glass of champagne, and her cigarettes.

I didn't resist. I sat down in the armchair and waited for her to fall asleep.

Calmer now than she seemed earlier, my grandmother stood up to greet me as I stepped into her room and wrapped her slender arms around me. A body was the only thing missing to give shape to her crepe dress, hanging in mid-air. The light was switched off, so I could barely make out her white hair.

'There... cry, my treasure. It's almost over. The journey is nearing its end. A different life awaits her, in another place. The only suffering she'll know will be yours, so you must be strong. You will let love in. The time has come for you to live your life as a woman. Olga, Freiga, Meyer, and Lev never resented me living. The past and its tormentors never eclipsed memories of us rolling around laughing, our round dances, our games. You will remember how grateful your mother was for your devotion, the strength of your bond. And you will forget all those little misunderstandings, the hopeless drunken nights, how she loved you so much she actually stopped you from living. You'll learn to understand her. You'll tame your memory and learn to read and interpret the signs that tell you she is there, close to you.

The time has come for you to be who you are. Go now, my treasure.'

# Gabriel

'Good evening, Jeanne.'

'Good evening Gabriel.'

'Aren't you afraid to come to a stranger's house like this?'

Jeanne's smile reminded me of her age.

'I trust you.'

'And you're right to - you could be my daughter.'

I poured her a glass of white wine, then took a seat in the armchair as she sat down on the sofa. She refused to hang her coat, setting it down on the floor instead, ready for a quick exit.

Hanging on the walls were pictures of tomatoes, courgettes, and aubergines (Blanche cared a great deal about her renowned vegetable patch).

Sitting there, Jeanne looked so frail. This wound she carried – I wanted to stop it bleeding. She dipped her lips in the wine glass, as a sparrow comes to drink from the cup of a waterlily.

'They say childhood is for building foundations. But what about teenage years? What role do they play in a life that is just starting? I'll tell you something, Gabriel: teenage years are for chasing pleasure, for tasting forbidden things. If you spend them well, they help you realise it's all pointless. They aren't the path that leads to adulthood; teenagers live a life within a life. You can get through it quickly by closing your eyes, or stop and take stock of all those first-times, building foundations. That first kiss, first tango, the first touch that sets off that pang in your stomach, right here. Give me your hand.'

I let her take my hand and place it there.

I pulled Jeanne towards me, forcefully. I inhaled her.

I took off her shoes, trousers, tee shirt. She covered herself with the shawl I'd left there to hide the sofa's worn armrest. I led her to one of the guestrooms, almost a replica of the one in which Hélène sleeps alone, not far from here, on the other side of Old Town.

I stroked her for a while, scanning her body. At my fingertips, the sparrow's breasts lifted upwards. I wanted her more than anyone. She was a piece in a puzzle and I was its neighbour; two parts that are meaningless until conjoined. In her, I felt wholeness for the first time.

Except I didn't know. How could I have known? She fell asleep. I watched her for a while, then left. I must never see her again. I'd never have made her happy. She wanted a different life, moments of pleasure I could never give her.

I abandoned Jeanne and the house, waiting long hours before returning. I sheltered from the darkness in a coffee shop where I sat and cried, my tears opening up a road I'd never walked down. From the trickle of a stream to the moans of the sea.

I never hid the truth from Hélène that Jeanne was too good for me.

# The day after

## Jeanne

The sun is rising over the sea. I'm back at the hotel. While she's asleep, I'll take a bath and pack my things. The flight is at midday. I'll wake her gently. A coffee, some grapefruit juice, the newspaper – wake up, mum.

The town is deserted. I feel the palms looking at me; I hear their murmurs, whispering secrets to one another. I walk along the hotel beach and feel the pebbles beneath my trainer soles. I long to touch the sea. The concierge hands me the key. I look into the lift mirror: I don't recognise myself, yet I'm the same as a few hours ago. Almost. I'm ten years behind everyone else. I open my bedroom door; the lights are off. The door between our rooms is open. She is sleeping. I collapse on my bed. I'm happy. Gabriel held me for a long time in his arms. Carefully, he unbuttoned my jeans, took off my tee shirt. Still smiling, Mickey ended up creased in a pile by the fireplace. Gabriel knelt beside me and untied my laces, but let me keep my red woollen socks because he could see I was shivering.

The fire went out. I was naked. He was dressed. He didn't even take off his shirt. I picked up my coat that I'd kept close by, then dumped it at the foot of the sofa. This coat is my shield, my chain-mail. A soldier never parts with what might save her life. And to protect myself from what I knew was coming, I wrapped myself in a rug I found draped over the sofa.

I was naked beneath a shroud, still wearing my red socks, in the middle of a living room that belonged to a man I didn't even know existed the day before.

He lay me down on the green sofa – the same velvet

that cushioned the many family reunions he talked about. He lifted the fabric covering my body and looked at me for a long time. He put his hand on my stomach, took me in his arms and carried me off to the bedroom, then set me down on the bed. I tried pulling the bedcover towards me as protection. He was gentle, not exactly tender, as he pulled it back towards him, dropped it outside, and closed the bedroom door, banishing its pattern of red and blue wilted flowers.

He sat on the bed, like a father tucking in his child, then leaned towards me and kissed me on the eyelids. His hands moved, one upwards, the other lower. As they spoke to me, my breath answered. He didn't take off his clothes. I felt him inside me, but I wasn't scared. Afterwards, he sat beside me and wiped away my tears. We didn't say a word. I fell asleep, cradled by his presence.

When I woke up at daybreak, I was alone. The living room was empty. I called out to Gabriel, but he was gone. I went back upstairs and stared at the tiny red stain on the vanilla bedcover in the guestroom. He had run away.

I picked up my black cloth knapsack, and as I left the house in the first rays of sun, I knew just what the trees where whispering.

Lying wide awake on my bed, I wonder: does Gabriel exist, or have I invented him? I order two breakfasts. She is still sleeping. We need to reach the airport in good time because I have to drop off the hire car. We will be back in Paris by early afternoon; I'll drop off my mother at her place, then have a few hours of normality before I meet her later for dinner. From now on I can't leave her alone for more than a few hours. I'm too afraid for her. She has seen nothing of the sea, nothing of Nice but the shadowy outlines of the palms.

I sneak into her room to wake her.

'Mum?'

No sound. Silence. I open the curtains.

I don't scream. I say nothing. This is the softest sleep you could ever imagine. Her face is relaxed. It seems to recognise something distant, shaping a smile.

Her glasses are on the bedside table. Her book is closed. The pillows are just as I'd arranged them last night. The champagne glass is empty, her cigarette packet untouched. Waiting for her in my room, coffee and grapefruit juice. And a pot of honey Colette had given us the other day.

I look at her for a while. I'm fully aware that she is dead, but don't understand why she isn't asking for her coffee. It isn't a shock; it's an end to torture. Hers? No, my own. I'd be lying if I said I was thinking about her in that moment. My Calvary has come to an end. An expected death, at first feared, then awaited. I take her hand; it's freezing. Of course it is – she is dead. But why is she cold? Because she is dead. Oh yes, right. I go back to my room. I sit down and wait. What am I waiting for? For her to wake up. But she won't wake up. She is dead. Oh right, yes. I go back over to her. From her window I see rows of palms, the sea, the street. I see cars and people. Nice doesn't know that a woman came to die at home, on its soil.

I can't smell her menthol cigarettes. It's funny because as soon as she wakes, lighting a cigarette is the first thing she does. I focus on the sea that looks nice and calm today, stroking its pebbled carpet. I know! I'll go and pick up a few stones before my flight, that way I can stack them on her bedside table in Paris. I close the window. I'm cold. I turn around. She looks pretty, asleep like that.

I think an hour went by before I called anyone. The emergency services came, a doctor, the hotel manager. Then the undertakers. I rang Colette who didn't give me a chance to speak: 'I'm on my way.'

Her door is closed now. The one that connects our rooms is locked for the moment. I don't understand all this fuss. For once, she is calm. I think of Gabriel; I wish he was here right now. I want him to undress me, to have me. I want to become tiny and sit in the palm of his hand so he can slip me in his pocket and carry me everywhere.

Colette tells me we have to dress my mother. Which trousers, which blouse for all eternity?

'I don't know! Why are you talking about eternity?'

I can't tell my mother now about meeting Gabriel. I can't tell her how complete I felt giving myself to this man, how happy it makes me that he was the first. Little by little, I make a list in my head of all the things I won't be able to tell her from now on. New love on the horizon, a dress that suits me, a hearty laugh, a dog lost and found, a marriage proposal, two blue lines on a pregnancy test, my son's eyes. A pain in the chest, adult acne, a friend's death, betrayal by another, my husband's tenderness, another two blue lines, my daughter's dimples.

That's when I crack. I've just glimpsed the start of eternity.

Facing the bed on which my mother is resting, my grandmother is sitting. This is the first time she has left her room since we arrived. Her travel bag is packed and ready beside her. She smiles as she plays with her pearl necklace.

'Don't you worry, my treasure – I'll stay by her side. I've come to collect her. I'll show her the way. She won't feel the cold; she will know no fear.'

# December 26<sup>th</sup>

## Gabriel

Exhausted from wandering, I came home that morning. The door was open and Jeanne had left. I hung up my worn-out overcoat and collapsed on same green sofa that had supported her tiny, naked frame hours earlier. I couldn't even get up to make coffee. Jeanne was everywhere. She was there, in the chair where I sat watching her curl up by the fireside, lying still at the foot of the sofa. The house still held her and would continue holding her for a long time.

'See, we are linked now. My walls watched that woman writhing in pleasure, giving you what others had been refused. My stones have sisters across town. We speak to each other often. Sun rays and crashing waves are our messengers. Do you know what the stones are saying? They say that a woman died in the night, just as Jeanne started living. They are talking about that woman. Don't cry, sisters: this woman came to die in the place she was born. And we watched her walk away into the distance, golden and glowing. By her bedside, Jeanne tried warming her. But they know that Jeanne's mother won't ever have to search for sleep again. So you see Gabriel, for Jeanne, her mother's death will be forever bound up in what she has given you. Dawn and dusk reunited.'

I looked at the vanilla bedcover in the guest room, then grabbed my coat, locked the house and left.

I knew I'd never come back to this house, except to show around potential buyers who would end up falling for its charms. I hoped Blanche would play her part by leaving the period-feature shutters alone, except the house seemed to blink of its own accord, terrifying would-be owners just before they sealed the deal.

Eventually it was sold to a couple, apparently unfazed by my aunt's otherworldly tricks. And Blanche did surrender in the end, but not before breaking a chandelier in the middle of their first night and stabbing the red velvet chaise longue with every fork in the house.

Fifteen years ago, I passed by with Hélène. I imagined ringing the bell, stepping inside, sitting down. Making peace with Blanche's ghost and asking the owners were they were happy there, within its walls?

No longer a house but a glass library without mystery.

Open to all, it gave everyone the chance to dive into an article, book, film, song, symphony. It was just then I decided to write this story, to once again set Jeanne down on the vanilla bedcover in that house, now vanished, to watch her come and fall asleep, far from what awaited her.

# *Epilogue*

## Jeanne

The plane passes over the motorway and lands. Journey's end. Having left for Nice with my mother and my grandmother's smile, now I was returning alone.

A short trip, original, a rite of passage: this has made me a woman, an orphan. I unlocked her apartment door and smelt her perfume in the air. Her beige coat was draped over one of the hallway armchairs. By its feet, a scarf. She must have deliberated over which one to wear before leaving.

I sat down in the living room with bright yellow walls and I waited. Waited for a sound, a sign of life. Nothing. Continued waiting. I lay down on the sofa, pulling the scattered cushions towards me. As I kept watch, I heard only the beating of my heart.

It was dark when I woke up. Wrapped up in my shawl, knees against my chest, hair stuck to my forehead, I swore I'd heard the sound of heels on the floorboards.

And her voice, so unique, gravelly from too many cigarettes, yet light from all the hoping, slight and shrinking from all the hiding from death. I hear her laugh, so immediate; an illusion so real it sets me off roaring. She is no lingering shadow; she isn't clinging to this world she just left. No – I know she's in her rightful place, wherever she is. For the longest time I'm angry with her for not visiting me. Whenever a lightbulb blows, floorboards creak, or a passing riverboat's lights flit across a painting she loved, I imagine she is speaking to me. I tell myself she wants me to know that it's only the visible world she has left behind.

So I change the lightbulbs that have a lifespan just like everything else, have the floorboards repaired to stop the creaking, acknowledge the necessary randomness of boats passing by, governed only by lapping waves of the Seine.

I slowly realise that in order to have access to her, memories are all I have left. From now on I must choose either to cherish or purge them. I won't help memories survive the passage of time, nor will I close off this open wound from stormy weather.

This aimless wandering lasted for a long time. Several weeks, a few months maybe. I lived at her place, slept in her bed, drank her wine, read her books. Put on her jumpers and coats. I brought her apartment to life in order to distract it. My easel beside the window, I painted the same view over and over: palms lining the water.

I played with her wigs: my turn to be blonde, redhead, brunette. I wore her prosthetic breast. I went out into the street with a third one under my jumper.

I had the feeling I was being constantly followed and so would turn around quickly, hoping to surprise the person trailing me. Of course, there was never anyone. Embarrassed every time, I'd adjust my wig and put my breast back in place.

One day, I decided – and this decision was final – to leave my name behind and to take hers instead.

And so Jeanne ceased to exist overnight. I no longer answered to it. It was my way of not outliving her.

At first, Gabriel was intertwined with my mother's death. One night I called out my lover's name, then in the morning came the image of a cold body. Gradually, the memory of our affair took a strange, obsessional turn. On every page in my sketchbook I drew Gabriel's face. At first realistically: his eyes, slim lips, thick hair. Then came the idea of photocopying the most true-to-life sketch, and I went to distribute them, sometimes forcefully in that way salespeople do, among the crowds filtering out of the high courts. Professionals and members of the public alike, everyone was given a copy. I looked for Gabriel everywhere. I loitered in corridors outside courtrooms hoping to surprise him, sat in the public gallery imagining it was him I was watching from behind, the gown hanging on his large frame. I looked everywhere for his lace-up shoes and his cufflinks.

It was exhausting. I drew him for his missing parts, not as he was when he brought me to life. His eyes have disappeared, his mouth too. His hair has vanished under my eraser. Eventually he became a pencil dot. But a dot at the centre of the page.

And life came back. I stopped living trapped between two ghosts. Amid the ruins, soft grass was growing. At first sparse, then thicker, I tended to it. I stopped seeing signs of life as a desecration of my mother's memory.

Five years passed. I loved other men who never knew Jeanne. But every day, looking at this dot on a sheet torn from a sketchbook, I thought of him.

I went back to Nice a few times. Not to reunite with the place where I had watched my mother die, but to make peace with the memory of the night it happened. I went looking for her house, but it always shied away from me, defying my sense of direction, deviating from whichever path I was walking. I even had to ask myself if it had ever really existed.

Then, one day, I decided to set off in search of a person, not a fantasy. To allow the dot to become a face. I added a few wrinkles, just as the police add years to sketched faces of missing children in an attempt to project their adult form. I decided to confront reality and let go of everything I'd imagined, hoped for, dreamt of. The time had come to give great-grandchildren to my grandmother, still sitting and waiting, playing impatiently with her pearls.

Was the meeting arranged by a tired angel, keen to pass on the torch to the living? Maybe.

I bumped into Gabriel one morning, out of nowhere,

outside my apartment building. He was rushing somewhere, yet still he recognised me and kissed me, as if embracing a ghost. We swapped numbers. I told him Jeanne had vanished, surrendered, sunk, whatever – she was gone. Without even a question, he called me by my new name.

We married. We had children. I carried on painting. In my landscapes there are smiling faces. Suns rise in my faces.

It was long ago. Today, I'm no longer sure exactly where Nice is, still I paint palms lit by the sea, tapering off in a line, green and thick, then blue and never-ending.

The world pulls away and I let go.

# Gabriel

I arrive home from another business trip. I'm back with Hélène; I like coming back to her. I open our apartment door: there she is, purposeful and quiet, sitting in the messy kitchen. She welcomes me: 'My love – you're home just in time to help me put up a painting!'

I still haven't taken off my scarf and put down my bag, yet here I am, already holding a hammer, clenching a wall-hook between my teeth. I hang yet another canvas splayed with tracks of red lines. At the end of each, a daub of blue paint. A way of punctuating these new, strange sentences, or proof that painting can capture time?

The work is complete in the sense it now hangs independently, but the concept itself is infinite. Hélène could easily extend its lines outside the frame, pulling them further. I half expect to come home one day and find all hanging canvases connected by lines stretching across the walls.

In the end I found myself loving her. Her frailty, her obsessions, her thoroughness. I decided to let go of Jeanne. I value the life that connects us, the way she has rubbed herself out to make more space for us all. Yet the lines that were once vanilla-coloured have turned clay-red and green.

When Hélène herself starts fading away, turning pastel, her canvases become all the more present.

Thirty years I've spent watching her draw and paint. In the beginning, the sea looked like the sea; I could tell whose face it was by the shape of the mouth. But slowly objects started to shrink back from their own form. Where at first I'd seen waves dancing in the eyes of those captured, later they were tidal.

Now I understand nothing of these flowing streams and coloured markings, nor the cocktail parties she organises twice a year, inviting friends to splash out on paintings – a pseudo business that taints her work with so-called value.

She has had her horizontal periods, her vertical ones. For the last ten years she has been caught in a diagonal cycle. The colours no longer blend; they avoid contact with one another, no longer communicate. I have tried to interpret these lines, big and small.

'These are my paths,' she tells me, smiling.

Hélène and me, these paths – it has been so long since we walked them together. Each on his or her own side, we would trace the lines of the frame to avoid brushing past one another.

At home, hundreds of lines now decorate the walls. There are monochrome paintings, too.

'But how can you see where the lines are when everything is blotted out in blue and red?'

'They are everywhere, of course! It's just – they are the same colour as the background.'

Today, the only paths she walks are those painted for herself.

I had internalised Jeanne somewhere deep within. And there she lived, in a place dark and secretive. In the early days spent with Hélène, it took a lot to drown out that voice in memory that came calling:

'Open up! It's me, Jeanne.'

'You can't come in.'

'I'm begging you.'

'You don't exist, not any more. I barely remember you.'

'Give me a chance! Only the living die. I won't bother you. I'll make myself small, tiny. You won't even know I'm there.'

'You chose to vanish. You can't go back on that now.'

I sometimes thought I'd invented our meeting, that Jeanne was a phantom born out of a fantasy.

Life went on: clients, courts, cases, pleas.

I stopped resisting my peers' self-branding. Even if gowns are still decorated here and there, I maintain that neutrality is what underpins equality in the courtroom. How can you accept a Legion of Honour? What makes any of us worthy?

That Christmas, in Nice, when I first met Jeanne – how bygone and unreal it seemed. A world apart, far from our planet. I had to listen closely to hear the voice of my sparrow, forever red-hatted and red-socked. If I focused for long enough it soothed me, picturing the curve of her breasts in my hands.

The same hands that have held leather gloves, opera tickets, books I'll never read, scarves I'll likely lose. And in the end they have forgotten the feel of Jeanne's breasts, her stomach.

I've been faithful to Hélène for so long now. I had no energy for infidelity. I became an honorary lawyer, called upon only rarely out of respect for my age and experience. At home we found a sort of morning serenity based not on joy or journeying further, but on understanding. Sometimes I was prepared to admit to myself, when my conscience came knocking, that I'd never made Hélène happy, that our life together was built on a chance meeting between a man who had already walked for long miles and a young woman taking her very first steps.

The further these coloured paths stretched, the more her life faded. She abandoned painting only when children and problems came calling. Tormentors. Love. Work. We had to be there, to listen to, feed and pamper them, insist they get home before bedtime. Feed them again, apologise for our terrible parenting. Sorrys at five, eight, fifteen. I'd been absent, unfaithful, distant, busy. Surrendering, I welcomed the blame. I guess I got used to being the guilty one, shouldering the responsibility for everyone's anxieties and failures.

I was alive without living.

We grew old, and Jeanne disappeared for good: her stomach, eyes, oversized coat, hands, voice, smile.

Hélène still paints, yet for the last few months, the only sight captured in her paintings are the walls of the specialist hospital she now lives in.

She doesn't know who I am. She doesn't recognise the twins; she calls them Meyer and Lev.

Further and further away she drifts. She talks to herself, sometimes singing a low tune in a language I don't understand.

Smiling, she tells me she is twenty-five, that life is calling out to her.

The other day, she asked if I would bring her blue coat and red hat.